EFFORTLESS WEIGHT LOSS AND FREEDOM FROM DIABETES

FREEDOM FROM DIABETES WITHOUT MEDICINE

VIJAY SHANKAR WADAGBALKAR

This book is dedicated to my Gurus , my family, my mentors, and the patients who have inspired me to pull the future of health close to those who need help today.

EAT TO LIVE

WE HELP MASSES TO LIVE MEDICINE FREE LIFE

Contents

Foreword

Happy and wealthy life starts with good health . When 1/3rd of India's population suffers from diabetes it's a serious problem. This book shares the step by step process of living a healthy life. Have known Mr Vijay Wadagbalkar as a wealth coach but his initiative to coach people on health with simple ideas and solutions is commendable . Best wishes to him and all his readers to live a healthy and wealthy life.

- Kanak Kr Jain , Volatility Coach & Author . founder SSL Academy

"Thanks to Vijay Wadagbalkar Ji, for your Healthy Lifestyle Formula Program, I am now free from 15 years of Diabetes and High BP medications. I have dropped 3 kg in a month and reduced waistline by 2 inches, and most importantly, my energy levels have improved substantially ."- Says Rotarian CA, Mr. Sharat Jain From Mumbai, India.

CA Sharat Jain,

Mumbai, India

Seema Vasudev corona exp 2020" We are indeed very grateful to Shri Vijay Wadagbalkar ji for having rendered selfless services during 2020 for his untiring efforts in guiding us to get out of carona fever with zero medicines under the able mentorship of Dr Biswaroop Chowdahary with a Team of 450+ NICE (Net work Of Influenza Experts) Experts , who were instrumental in curing 50,000 carona patients with zero medicines, zero hospitalization and zero mortality and zero fees. I , Seema Vasudev mother of Atul Vasudev, (11 Years son of mine) got cured out of carona fever in August 2020 and express my sincere gratitude to Shree Vijay Wadagbalkar ji and Entire NICE Team for their Selfless Services-"

Seema Vasudev, Srirampur, Madhya Pradesh.

Preface

I was suffering from being overweight by 10 kg and was suffering from Diabetes and was in search of a permanent solution to both these problems. In addition, I saw both my mother , a very close friend dying due to severe Diabetes complications.

Hello, I am Vijay Wadagbalkar, Healthy Lifestyle & Abundance Expert from Mumbai. I am a Diabetes Educator from Indo -Vietnam Medical Board and also a Network of Influenza Care Expert (NICE).

.

At age 40 I was overweight by 10 kilos and for 20 years I was struggling to lose that extra 10 kilos, on the contrary I got additional 5 kilos. Thus, at age 60 I was overweight by 15 kgs. However, the day I found the formula for weight loss, within 6 months I lost 10 killers and 5 inches on my waist line and I have maintained that for the last 5 years. it's because I understood the meaning of diet that is a Latin word which means a way of life whatever you can do for rest of your life that only you should eat as a food which is a right food and from that day it's my passion to help someone who is overweight or obese, to help him reduce that extra Pounds on his body by prescribing the right food as a diet plan to him and her. That is how we have helped hundreds of people lose extra weight and that formula I am going to share in my book.

The second challenge I was facing at my age 58 was type 2 diabetes. I was advised by my family physician to take ecosprin AV 75, a blood thinner tablet stating that I will never get a heart attack or a stroke. But within 12 months, I got a free gift of two diseases 1 high blood pressure and 2. type 2 diabetes. For 4 years continuously, I was taking 5 tablets a day for my high blood pressure ,gout , and thyroid problem and type 2 diabetes. I used to always ask my family physician why the power of medicine was increasing month after month and my immunity was going down. My doctor used to react saying I will have to take metformin and bp tablets till my last breath. It did not appeal to me and I challenged my family physician that one day, I will bring a solution to the table for reversing my type 2 diabetes as I told him that I am not born with blood pressure and diabetes. both these are lifestyle related diseases, which should get cured if I change my lifestyle.

That is how in 2018, I ultimately found a solution for reversal of type 2 diabetes and weight loss. My journey started with the able guidance of Dr Jagannath Dixit from Latur. I started my two meals diet plan and within six months I lost 9 kg and also lost 4 inches on my waistline. Then I came across YouTube videos of Dr Biswaroop Chaudhary, whose concept of DIP DIET (DISCIPLINED INDIVIDUAL PERSON) Eating lots of fresh raw vegetables and fruits appealed to my reason and I then attend it in March 2019 4 day International Conference at Naturopathy College in Bhopal conducted by Dr Bishwaroop Chowdhary and also attended by Dr Bimal Chajjar, heart surgeon from Delhi.In those 4 days in the company of Dr Biswaroop Roy Chowdhury I learnt the technique of how eating right food becomes medicine and you don't need to eat medicine separately.

On the last day of the seminar I RESOLVED to start my journey as Health Care Professional and my mission now is to help million people to Inspire, Educate and Empower to live Medicine-Free Life by changing three areas of their life, viz., Breath , Eating and Thinking so that they can live a happy, healthy, peaceful and financially free life and medicine free life

And one of the ways to inspire, Educate and Empower million people is to write an ebook titled "Effortless weight-loss and Freedom from Type2 Diabetes. I am very confident that you readers would find the concepts , methods and solutions given are very simple and very effective in weight reduction and freedom from Type2 Diabetes.

Cheers,
Vijay Wadagbalkar
Health Coach
Mumbai , 28th May, 2022.

"Our Mission is to Inspire, Educate and Empower 100.000 people to live Medicine Free Life" VIJAY WADAGBALKAR

CHAPTER ONE

Chapter 1-ABC Of Good Health

Before we talk about what is type 2 diabetes and myths about type 2 diabetes I would like to share with you the basic care which is required to be taken by every individual who is seeking good health.

One must monitor or a six monthly basis or at least once in a year especially after the age of 40 the following four numbers which I call all as ABC of good health. and they are are your hba1c(that is 3 months average blood sugar), secondly you must know your blood pressure you must know your total cholesterol level and breakup of what is your good cholesterol , I.e. HDL and what is your bad cholesterol, LDL what is your triglycerides number and the ratio between HDL and triglycerides should be 1:2. In Other words , if your HDL is equal to or more than 40, then your triglycerides should not be more than 80. This is a parameter for good healthy heart. You must check your weight regularly to make sure your BMI =>25. Example , If your height is 170 cm, then your weight should not exceed 70 Kgs.

I give below 9 questions to ask about yourself,Which are indicators of good health. Absence of disease does not mean you have good health.

Question number 1:

Do you have a uniform body temperature in other words you do not your legs and feet do not become cold air your head doesn't become cold. but there is a uniform body temperature that is a sign of good health.

Question number 2:

Did you feel your body was lighter and not heavy, then it's a sign of good health if not it means you're eating heavy food aur fast food. then the solution for you is practice intermittent fasting.

Question number 3:

Are you experiencing joy or in other words are you feeling good all through 24 hours. If yes it's a sign of good health.

Question number 4:

Do you get a natural hunger if yes it is a sign of good health. if not drink one and a quarter liter of water early in the morning when you wake up.

Question number 5:

Are you getting a good night's sleep if yes it is a sign of good health .

Question number 6 :

Are you happy from within or are you feeling that you are experiencing happiness in your mind for 24 hours? It's a sign of good health.

Question number 7:

Does your body's signaling system work perfectly in order?. If not the reason is overdose of allopathic medicine resulting in inflammation in endothelium cells of your blood. The solution is easy on the right food.

Question number 8:

Do you feel enthusiasm in carrying out any of your work or task during the day? In other words you do not feel laziness. If not, this solution is to eat a whole food plant based diet with less salt oil and sugar.

Question number 9:

Is your body's excretory system functioning properly? For example, are you passing stool normally in the morning without having a cup of tea or coffee.If not, eat a whole food plant based diet and drink One And ¼ liter water early in the morning when you wake up.

CHAPTER TWO

Chapter 2: What is Type2 Diabetes?

Hello, we're going to talk about what is type 2 diabetes

2. Type 2 diabetes is not a disease but it is a metabolic syndrome disorder. In other words, metabolic syndrome disorder can be reversed by changes in your lifestyle that is the way you breath, the way you eat, the kind of food you eat, the way you exercise, the way you sleep or the quality of your sleep and the way you think. Therefore diabetes reversal can be handled by the changes in your breath , Eating the right food, doing exercises on a regular basis and reducing stress by thinking positively.

Understand what is type 2 diabetes and why is it caused?

3. If you understand the term insulin resistance then you will understand what type 2 diabetes is. I will explain to you at a cellular level how the insulin resistance in the human body cell is caused due to the wrong kind of food we eat by having a close look at the picture given below, I have drawn a picture of a cell. In the cell you can clearly see on the right hand side there are two or three insulin keys in red color , whereas On the right hand side you can see a picture of 7-8 fats in yellow color. When the carbohydrate or sugar enters in the cell at the receptor of Insulin key, what happens is that the fat (in yellow color) in the cell acts like chewing gum and blocks the entry of carbohydrate entering into the key, called insulin . Therefore , what happens is the insulin receptor key is blocked by excess fat in the cell which acts like a chew in gum . This

is called insulin resistance.

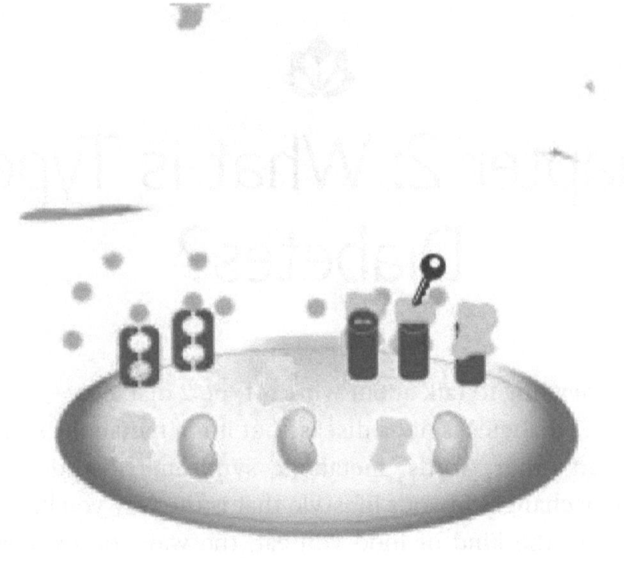

Enter Caption

5. Therefore, if you understand the problem is not lack of insulin but insulin does not function normally due to excessive fat present in the cell. The solution therefore lies in removal of excess fat from the body at a cellular level. and therefore all you need to do is to eat less of fat by removing excessive fatty foods from your diet. So therefore, eliminate all animal products such as meat, chicken , fish including milk and milk products and eat less of salt, oil and sugar in your daily diet and you eat more of a whole food plant based diet, Which consists of more fiber and less fat and which also increases metabolism of the body, causing weight loss in the long run long term. It is therefore recommended to eat whole food plant based diet and eliminate from your diet animal products such as meat chicken , fish, and milk and Milk products and also consume minimum of oil so that insulin sensitivity improves and this is ultimate solution for reversal of type 2 diabetes which has been tried and tested for over 50 years and gives hundred percent result to everyone who adopts eating the whole food plant based diet with minimum oil .

6. In addition to eating the right food 50 lots of RAW vegetables and fruits one needs to also improve the quality of reading by practicing spiritual breathing exercises and also practicing meditation so as to reduce the stress levels and help reversal of type 2 diabetes by optimizing or reduction of body weight at the same time.

CHAPTER THREE

Chapter 3: What are the root causes of Type2 Diabetes ?

Type 2 diabetes is primarily the result of two interrelated problems:

1.· Cells in muscle, fat and the liver become resistant to insulin. Because these cells don't interact in a normal way with insulin, they don't take in enough sugar.

· 2. The pancreas is unable to produce enough insulin to manage blood sugar levels.

Although not everyone with type 2 diabetes is overweight, obesity and an inactive lifestyle are two of the most common causes of type 2 diabetes.

These things are responsible for about 90% to 95% of diabetes cases across India and across the Globe.

What Causes Type 2 Diabetes?

When you're healthy, your pancreas (an organ behind your stomach) releases insulin to help your body store and use sugar from the food you eat. Diabetes happens when one or more of the following occurs:

· Your pancreas doesn't make any insulin.

· Your pancreas makes very little insulin.

· Your body doesn't respond the way it should to insulin

Unlike people with type 1 diabetes, people with type 2 diabetes make insulin. But the insulin their pancreas releases isn't enough, or their body can't recognize the insulin and use it properly. (Doctors call this insulin resistance.)

When there isn't enough insulin or the insulin isn't used as it should be, glucose (sugar) can't get into your cells. It builds up in your bloodstream instead. This can damage many areas of the body. Also, since cells aren't getting the glucose they need, they don't work the way they should.

Risk Factors for Type 2 Diabetes:

Type 2 diabetes is believed to have a strong genetic link, meaning that it tends to run in families. If you have a parent, brother, or sister who has it, your chances rise. Several genes may be related to type 2 diabetes. Ask your doctor about a diabetes test if you have any of the following risk factors:

· High blood pressure

· High blood triglyceride (fat) levels. It's too high if it's over 150 milligrams per deciliter (mg/dL).

· Low "good" cholesterol level. It's too low if it's less than 40 mg/dL.

· Gestational diabetes or giving birth to a baby weighing more than 9 pounds

· Prediabetes. That means your blood sugar level is above normal, but you don't have the disease yet.

· Heart disease

· High-fat and carbohydrate diet. This can sometimes be the result of food insecurity, when you don't have access to enough healthy food.

· High alcohol intake

· Sedentary lifestyle

· Obesity or being overweight

· Polycystic ovary syndrome (PCOS)

· You're over 45 years of age. Older age is a significant risk factor for type 2 diabetes. The risk of type 2 diabetes begins to rise significantly around age 45 and rises considerably after age 65.

· A proper diet and healthy lifestyle habits such as Breath right, Eat the right food, exercise right, and think right or think positively , along with medication, if you need it, can help you reverse type 2 diabetes.

CHAPTER FOUR

Chapter 4:Empower Your Breath and Thought - Your Key to Health & Success

Every human being is potentially *Divine*. Hence he/she has within him/her all the power required to achieve success or to overcome his/her difficulties and problems.

The *Laws of Life* operate through *Breath* and *Thought*. Brahmavidya gives definite methods by which a person can overcome all his physical & mental problems and lead a healthier, happier and more successful life. The methods are simple yet very effective. By *Right Breathing & Right Thinking*, we harmonize our energy and resources to achieve desired results on all the three levels of our existence viz. physical, mental & spiritual.

Let us resolve the right to join Brahmavidya Basic Course to learn and practice 8 spiritual breathing exercises and meditation and make the practice a new habit to empower your Breath and Thought!!! Visit:https://Brahmavidya.net

CHAPTER FIVE

Chapter 5: Home Remedy for Corona Fever Cure

Are you Corona Positive?

Don't panic . Follow the following simple 10 steps (proven home remedy which has given 100% success in every single case with zero side effects) -:

Do not take any tablets (allopathic or homeopathy) to get relief for fever or body pain.

Take hot water steam and gargle with warm water (put half spoon of turmeric powder in the water) TWICE a day , once after you get up in the morning and secondly, before you go to bed at night .

Day 1-: (Liquid diet) Take tender coconut water and Orange or Mosambi juice (vitamin c)

How much quantity? If your weight is 60 kg then 60/10+6 glasses (250 ml glass) 6 glasses of coconut water and 6 glasses of orange juice (alternatively). One glass of water in between if you are thirsty. 1st full day only liquid diet as above.

Day 2-: (Semi solid and liquid diet) Take tender coconut water and Orange or Mosambi juice (vitamin c)

How much quantity? If your weight is 60 kg then 60/20 = 3 glasses (250 ml glass) 6 glasses of coconut water and 3 glasses of orange juice (alternatively). One glass of water in between if you are thirsty.

At 12PM-1PM, and evening 7PM and 8 PM take cucumber and tomato slides as salad(60*5=300 grams).

Day 3 -:(Semi solid and liquid diet) Take tender coconut water and Orange or Mosambi juice (vitamin c).

How much quantity? If your weight is 60 kg then 60/30 = 2 glasses (250 ml glass) 2 glasses of coconut water and 2 glasses of orange juice (alternatively). One glass of water in between if you are thirsty.

At 12PM-1PM, and evening 7PM and 8 PM take cucumber and tomato slides as salad.(60*5=300 grams)

By 4PM on the 3rd day , your body temperature would become normal and so also your Body's Energy levels.

In the night, for dinner , strat with tomato and cucumber and then have your normal cooked food.

By following the above process, we as a TEAM of 750 Network of Influenza Care (NICE) Experts have cured 60,000 corona+ve cases with zero medicines, zero hospitalization, zero mortality and zero fees under the guidance of Dr Biswaroop Choudhary.

CHAPTER SIX

Chapter 6: Amazing Healing Capacity of the Human Body

1. Hippocrates, the Father of Modern Medicine has said" Doctors of the future will not human body with medicine but food thy be medicine".He also said further "You are a fool if you don't become your own Doctor .

2. In Brahmavidya , Human body has been described as "Transcendally Beautiful, Infinitely Intricate and Most Gloriously Accurate Instrument in the Universe.

3. Considering the infinite potential of the Human Body to heal by itself, let us together build a Healthy Lifestyle Community by living the above message of Hippocrates and let's together make a world more happier, healthier and peaceful by Eating The Right Foods and thus living medicine free life.

CHAPTER SEVEN

Chapter 7: Intermittent Fasting prevents Cancer!!!

IMPORTANCE OF INTERMITTENT FASTING IN HEALING CANCER:

The human body is capable of protecting itself from cancer. Each T cell has the power to kill 1000 cancer cells.

But we, with our wrong food habits , sleeping habits and waking up and other wrong habits, we have suppressed the power of T cells.

But, do you want to know how this power comes to you? Earlier we used to have radiation, then came chemotherapy and now we have immunotherapy.

Immunotherapy, where you be each T cell I'm repeating the two doctors, Dr Hunza and Dr Ellison, who got 2018 Nobel prize for Medicine to say that, if you do a waterless fast, that is not where you were sleeping okay at night while you're awake and you are in the midst of activity ID for 20 days in a year then there is least chances of your body getting affected by cancer.

CHAPTER EIGHT

Chapter 8:Eating the right food, so food becomes medicine.

Simple steps to reverse Diabetes in 72 hours

Steps to design your Whole Food Plant Based Diet

EAT THE RIGHT FOOD SO FOOD BECOMES MEDICINE.

Step number 1:

Between 8 AM and 12 noon ,eat only three to four types such as apple, per, pomegranate, watermelon ,Kiwi fruit, papaya, oranges, that is fruits having lower glycemic index.

Minimum quantity to be consumed is equal to your body weight in kg x 10 is equal to 2 in grams.

For example if your body weight is 70 kgs,then you should eat 700 grams of fruits 12 noon.

Step number 2:

Always eat your lunch and dinner in two plates **plate number 1 and plate number 2** as under-:

Plate 1 : Should consist mainly of salad consisting of 4 types of RAW vegetables cucumber tomato, curry leaves, Methi leaves,Carrot, beetroot, extra etc.

for example if your

Weight is 70 kilos then you should read 350 grams of raw vegetables as salad in each of your meals i.e lunch as well as dinner.

Plate number 2:After you finish eating plate number 1 then you can have home cooked vegetarian food consisting of cooked vegetables, dal rice chapati chutney etc.

The rules for lunch and dinner are the same however one must remember to try to finish dinner by 7 p.m.

Step number 3:AVOID

1.Animal food including Milk products.

2. Multivitamin tonic and capsules

3. Refined and Packed food.

Other than threeeals of breakfast lunch and dinner following are the options for snacks-:

1. sprouts body weight in kgs= ....grams.

2.Seeds such as Almonds, Walnut ,pistas. Not exceeding 70 grams if your weight is 70 kilos.

3.Fruits can also be consumed as snacks.

4. Fresh coconut water ke naam se bataye

5. Hunza Tea.

The above diet will help you lower your blood sugar levels. You are advised to keep tapering the tablets and insulin dose so as to avoid hyperglycemia.

The above diet is a sure shot way to keep medicines away permanently provided the above diet becomes a permanent part of your lifestyle except with the exception of Vocational cheating especially when you go out on a marriage party etc. Cheating is allowed only once in 3 weeks and not more. This is the only way to remain healthy and prevent future occurrence of diabetes or hypertensive condition or even heart disease.

The solution to attract good health and eliminate all chronic diseases lies in adopting sattvic lifestyle-:

Two Sattvic Meals a day Plan for 3 weeks-:

At 8:00 a.m. in the morning take Detox juice coconut water or Ash gourd juice or Vegetable juice .

At 9 a.m. :Go for a 40 to 60 minutes brisk walk, swimming, cycling or Surya Namaskar . it is absolute must to do an exercise in the morning or else do it in the evening

At 10:00 a.m. have breakfast A ball of local and regional fresh fruit .

At 1 p.m. have your lunch.

2-3 satvik rotis prepared with the starchy vegetables such as potato sweet potato pumpkin are prepared in a Satvik way.

At 7:00 p.m. have your dinner. Salad or Soup.

If having soup , have a bowl of sweet potato alongside, if having a salad, have a handful of soaked nuts alongside.

Do 16 hours fasting everyday Nature"s supreme Medicine.

Taking a sunbath for 20 minutes everyday is the best disinfectant.

CHAPTER NINE

Chapter 9: Eat lots of fruit for Breakfast (between 8 AM and 12 noon).

It's highly recommended that you eat 4to 5 types of different colored fruits for brea-fast locally or regionally grown fruits in your area like Per, Pomegranate, Apple, Banana, Mangoes, Grapes, Watermelon, etc.

Here we have listed the top 20 fruits that can be eaten by diabetics...

Many times a question is asked in my Workshops , Weather Diabetics can eat sweet fruits like banana, Chiku, Grapes and mangoes?

And the good news is yes you can eat mangoes or any sweet fruits for that purpose, as it contains fructose which is not soluble in blood and therefore blood glucose does not go up after conception of mangoes. It has been Dhruv in a randomized control trial as reported in New Journal of Nutritional Science (JNS)(2017) Vol6e59 Page 1 of 15 that after consumption of fruit juice by a group of 1800+ diabetic people after 2 hours their blood glucose level did not go up aur ise then what it was before the conjunction of the fruit juice in other words, there is no adverse effect on the blue blood glucose level after consumption of sweet fruits.

Here is a **list of 20 Fruits a Diabetic can consume for a breakfast :**

Pears :

Rich in vitamins and fiber, this delicious food is one of the healthier snacking options for diabetics.

Papaya :

Another 'super-food' for diabetics is papaya. Papaya contains essential minerals and vitamins, hence, can be eaten by people suffering from diabetes.

Starfruit :

Somewhat similar to jamuns, starfruit is another option for diabetics. It controls your blood sugar level but in case a person has diabetes nephropathy, starfruit should be avoided.

Guava :

Guava is good for controlling blood sugar and also prevents constipation. Loaded with vitamin A and C, they also contain high dietary fiber.

Kiwi fruit :

You could include kiwi in your diet. Many researchers have proved that eating kiwis could actually help you in lowering your blood sugar levels.

Black Jamun :

This fruit is one of the best fruits for people suffering from diabetes. It not only controls your blood sugar level but also helps in controlling diabetes.

White Jamun or Wax Jambu:

Enriched with fiber, white jamuns help in controlling blood sugar levels. Hence, they are great for people suffering with diabetes.

Cherries :

Cherries are considered as a healthy snack for diabetic people as their GI (Glycemic Index) value is 20 and in some cases, even less than 20.

Peaches :

Peaches also have low GI value, hence this is a great and healthy treat for people suffering from diabetes.

Berries :

Berries are available in different varieties. All berries are loaded with antioxidants and keep your sugar level in check. You can eat strawberries, raspberries, blackcurrants, chokeberries, cranberries and acai berries. All these varieties are good for diabetics.

Apples :

Apples are enriched with antioxidants which help in reducing cholesterol level, improve digestive system and boost immunity. Apples also contain essential nutrients which helps in easy digestion of fats.

Pineapples :

Pineapples are rich in anti-viral, anti-inflammatory and have antibacterial properties. They are good for people suffering from diabetes.

Figs :

As figs are loaded with fiber, they help with proper insulin function in diabetes patients.

Oranges :

Loaded with vitamin C, this citrus fruit can be consumed daily by diabetic people.

Watermelon :

Though watermelons contain high GI value, their glycemic load is low. This makes it a good and healthier food option for diabetic patients. But, it is advised that you should have watermelon in moderation.

Grapefruit :

Grapefruit helps in controlling the blood sugar level. So, including them in your diet is a good option to control diabetes.

Pomegranate :

The tiny red pearls are great for diabetic people as they help in improving their blood sugar level.

Cantaloupe :

Another great fruit option for diabetics is cantaloupe. Cantaloupe contains high GI but is also loaded with a good amount of fiber. Hence, eating them in moderation is healthy for diabetic people.

Jackfruit :

Loaded with vitamin A, vitamin C, niacin, calcium, thiamin, riboflavin, potassium, iron, magnesium, manganese and many other essential nutrients, jackfruit is another healthier option for diabetics. Jackfruit also improves insulin resistance in diabetic people.

Amla :

Amla is also referred to as 'super-food' for diabetic people. Amla is rich in vitamin C and fiber, hence, can be added in your daily diet.

NOTE: It should be noted that if you have diabetes, before adding any fruit in your diet, kindly consult your doctor.

CHAPTER TEN

Chapter 10: Medicine"s adverse effect on liver

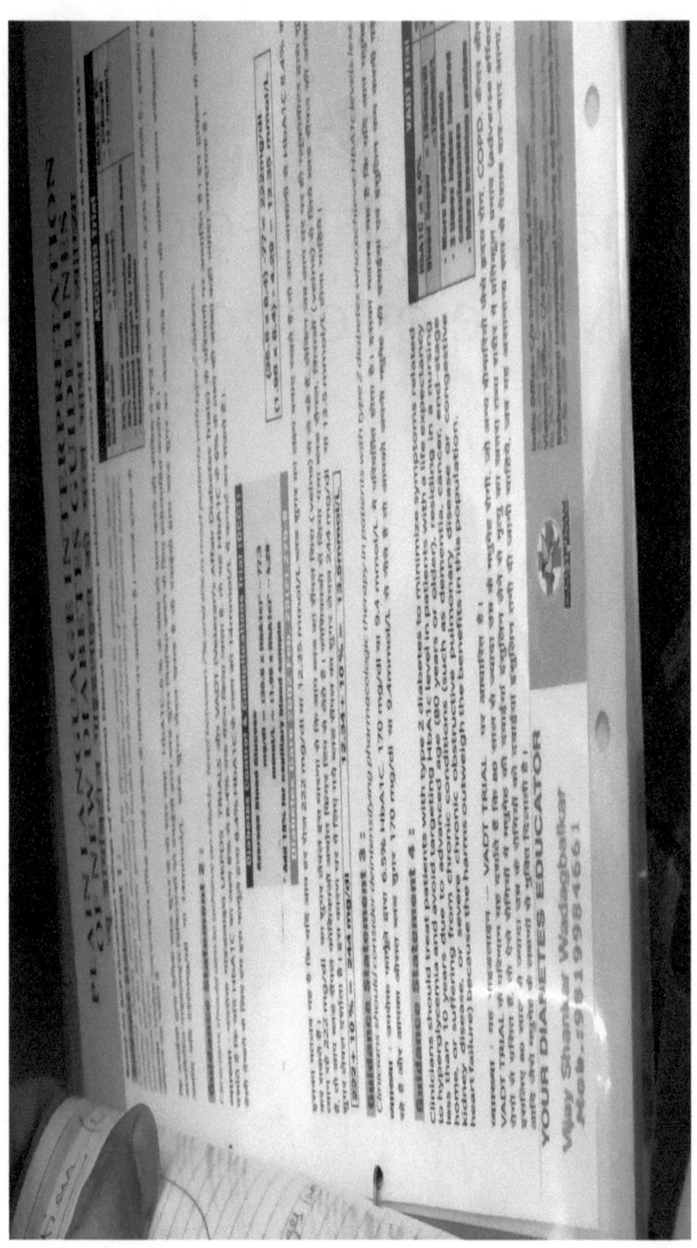

ACP GUIDELINES ON DIABETES DATED 06.03.2018

American College of physicians had issued New Diabetes Guideline dated 6th of March 2018, the summary of which is as shown in the above picture. Which clearly states that high blood sugar is bad but reducing the blood sugar by medication such as metformin or insulin is worst. In terms of ACCORD TRIAL, it has been pointed out that That overdose of medicine leads to 22% closer to death; 38% more cardiovascular related death; increase in weight by 10 kilos and increased fluid retention.

Therefore, utmost care should be taken, especially individuals in the age group of 60 to 80 before they take recourse to medicine to reduce their higher blood sugar level.

CHAPTER ELEVEN

SNAKE & LADDER GAME

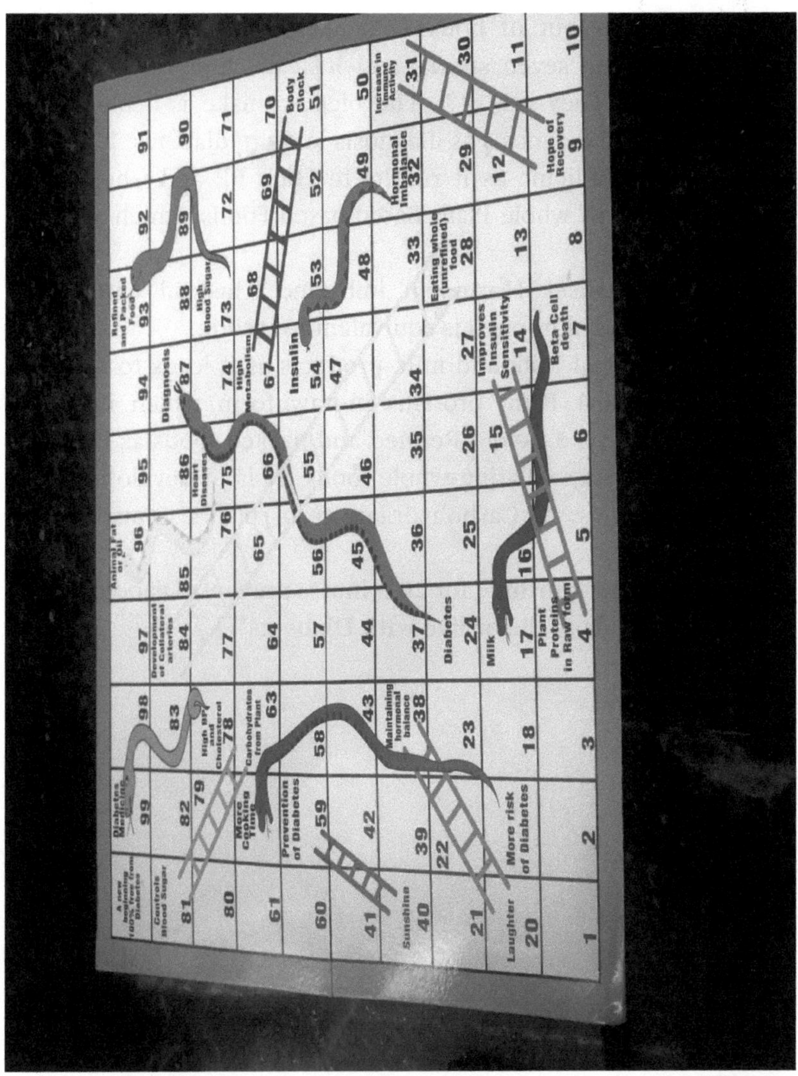

SNAKE & LADDER GAME

If you want to live a disease free life and medicine free life all you need to do is convert Your kitchen into a Mini Hospital and convert your masala box in the kitchen into a medicine box and follow these simple rules under-:

Rule 1:Throw out of house 7 snakes so as to avoid getting swallowed by the seven snacks and instead climb all 7 Ladders in the picture. They are -: 1. The biggest snake is a blue one , Diagnosis. Avoid diagnosis as diagnosis leads to diabetes. 2. Do not take diabetes medicine as it results in High BP and Cholesterol. Instead Eat lots of whole Plant Based based Foods, which acts as a medicine.

3. Insulin causes Hormonal imbalance, instead eating raw vegetables as its chlorophyll is equivalent to insulin.

4.Avoid Animal Milk and milk products as it leads to beta cell death, instead eat Plant proteins in raw form which improves insulin sensitivity. 5. Avoid Refined and packed foods as it results in High Blood Sugar. Eating whole foods leads to development of Collateral arteries. 6. Carbohydrates from plants control blood sugar.

7. Being under sunshine for 20 minutes prevents Diabetes.

"No one needs to die or live with Diabetes"

CHAPTER TWELVE

Super green smoothie recipe

Chapter 12 : Super Green Smoothie for weight loss and as a substitute for metformin tablets/insulin.

Super green smoothie recipe:

1to 2 glass of water about 250 ml

Take dalchini or cinnamon powder, curcumin powder, Himalayan salt for black salt black pepper 1 teaspoon each of his power.

Then take relieves of 5 to 10 curry leaves, 2to 5 pudina leaves, 2-3 nagveli leaves and 5 to 6 Tulsi leaves,

Thereafter, add one fruit Idea Apple vah vah tomato banana mosambi for pumpkin.

Take all the above ingredients and put them in the grinder for 2 to 3 minutes.

Our super green smoothie is ready for drinking. Not bi feature and one should have at least two 250 ml glass, one in the one in the empty stomach early in the morning before 7:30 a.m. and second at 4:30 p.m. in the afternoon you can keep this in the refrigerator.

This way start with Two glasses of super green smoothie a day And then gradually increase everyday MI A1 glass so that at the end of the week you are consuming six classes of super Greens movie 1250ml., which will ensure Effortless Weight loss and reduction of blood sugar level to normal levels.

Conclusion:

Green Smoothie= Chlorophyll= Insulin , so taking Super Green Smoothie (500 ml=2 glasses) twice a day once in the morning at 7.30 AM. And secondly, in the afternoon at 4.30 PM will certainly help get rid of excess body weight as well as metformin tablets/ insulin dose.

"LIVE HEALTHY , LIVE MEDICINE FREE LIFE".

CHAPTER THIRTEEN

Happiness Dose

Happiness Dose

My dear readers, if you do anything, being happy is your first duty to yourself. My learning arising out of Brahma Vidya please always be happy and give thanks.

I am now going to share with you a piece of knowledge, which if implemented is a real power.One of the main causes of type 2 diabetes is the level of stress or anxiety which causes this Lifestyle disorder. In other words your mind plays a very important role and by being a student of Brahma Vidya if you religiously and regularly practice its spiritual breathing exercises and meditation for at least 20 to 25 minutes every single day then you will be able to release four happy chemicals in your brain . They are dopamine ,Oxytocin, serotonin and endorphin. as against this and Audi man has increased levels of unhappy chemicals viz., cortisol and adrenaline which are the stress hormones.

Let me elaborate on these four happy hormones, more so that you can make sure that you release these four happy hormones on a daily basis so that they will help you achieve your BIGGER GOALS in Life. .

Dopamine: If you have any good or bad habit example you love a cup of coffee or you love eating pizza so when you have that cup of coffee in addition to pizza you feel very happy this is exactly what dopamine is all about.

Oxytocin:

Oxytocin means if you touch your loved one with love Oxytocin chemical is released in the body. The classic example of Oxytocin is when a mother touches a happy baby at that moment of time.

serotonin: when you help others you are releasing serotonin in your body. how happy I was when I got my first 9 students for Brahma Vidya how happy I was when CS Girish Nadkarni call me to inform that he has been very very happy to join Brahma with their basic force 5 years back on my recommendation and today he is pursuing final the perceptor levels for teachers training course in Brahma Vidya. The moral of the stories is to go out of your way and help others and get blessings from others.

Endorphin:

This happiness hormone is released in the brain when you achieve any of your Goals, for example, if I decide to go for a brisk walk for 40 minutes and I do that for two consecutive weeks without fail, how happy will I be and like that you make sure that you have more and more endorphin moments in your life on every day, every week, every month, and every year by setting a particular goal and achieving that goal. Some of my endorphin moments are as under -:

When I passed my Company Secretaries Final Exam in June 1978;

When I got my 1st 9 students for Brahmavidya Basic Course.

When I became Grandfather .

How to ensure that the above 4 happy hormones are released on a daily basis.?

If you practice 5 minutes breathing exercise early morning , in particular, 300 strokes of Bhastrika in a standing pose (listen to Baba Ramdev's youtube video on the subject., your body will release 24 hours these 4 happy hormones and your cortisol and adrenaline levels will drop so your stress will be replaced by happiness.

Printed by Libri Plureos GmbH in Hamburg,
Germany